THE SECRET DIARY OF Kitty Cask

Illustrated by
Jamie Littler

Philip Ardagh

SMUGGLER'S DAUGHTER

WITHDRAWN FROM STOCK

D0307640

First published in the UK in 2019 by Nosy Crow Ltd
The Crow's Nest, Baden Place, Crosby Row
London, SE1 1YW, UK

The words 'The National Trust' and the oak leaf logo are registered trademarks of the
National Trust for England, Wales and Northern Ireland used under licence from
National Trust (Enterprises) Limited (Registered Company Number 01083105).

Nosy Crow and associated logos are trademarks and/or
registered trademarks of Nosy Crow Ltd

Text copyright © Philip Ardagh, 2019
Illustrations © Jamie Littler, 2019

The right of Philip Ardagh and Jamie Littler to be identified as the author
and illustrator respectively of this work has been asserted by them in accordance
with the Copyright, Designs and Patents Act 1988.

A CIP catalogue record for this book will be available from the British Library

All rights reserved

1 3 5 7 9 10 8 6 4 2

This book is sold subject to the condition that it shall not, by way of trade
or otherwise, be lent, hired out or otherwise circulated in any form of
binding or cover other than that in which it is published. No part of this
publication may be reproduced, stored in a retrieval system,
or transmitted in any form or by any means (electronic, mechanical,
photocopying, recording or otherwise) without the prior
written permission of Nosy Crow Ltd.

Printed and bound in Great Britain by Clays Ltd, Elcograf S.p.A.

Papers used by Nosy Crow are made from wood grown in sustainable forests.

ISBN: 978 1 78800 057 4

www.nosycrow.com

Day 1

My name is Kitty Cask. That's Kitty short for Katherine with a 'K', but I've never had anyone call me by that name. My home is in Cornwall[1], and it's one of a cluster of cottages clinging to the hillsides in the village of Minnock where the river flows out into the English Channel.

---

1   Cornwall is the most westerly county in England, with the county of Devon its immediate neighbour to the east. Sticking out into the sea, it has the North Atlantic Ocean on its northern shores and the English Channel on its southern.

The French call the Channel 'La Manche', because they think the strip of water looks like a coat sleeve. Trust them to think of fashion! A Frenchie[2] is more interested in the cut of his trousers than in ruling the waves! It'll always be the English Channel, 'cause it's OUR sea, though calling it the Cornish Channel would be better still! Sometimes angry, with raging white waters, it tosses aside boats like my little sister, Esme, throws her toys from her cradle, wind howling like when Esme has a tooth comin' through. But, more often than not, it is our friend and provider, even if it can never be tamed.

Most of us living in these parts earn our daily bread[3] from the sea. My father says that's because very little of Cornwall is more than a day's walk from the coast, "so long you don't

---

2   The French had been traditional enemies and rivals of the English (and Cornish*) for many centuries.
*Many Cornishmen (and women) saw – and see – Cornwall as separate to the rest of England.

3   Not literally bread, of course. Fishing, trading and – in this instance – some rather illegal activities.

turn right and end in Devonshire!"[4]. These are exciting times, so I've decided to keep a diary of all that's occurring; putting on paper my thoughts and memories and the comings and goings in our village by the waves.

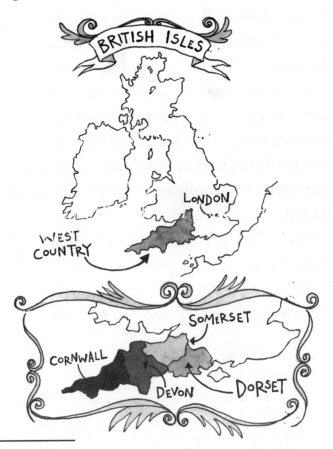

Day 2

Most of our menfolk are fishermen or work the tin mines[5] with the knockers[6], but mining is seasonal work, so many miners turn their hands to other things when needs must. Then there are those amongst us who do not belong: the King's men. These are the redcoats[7] and the excisemen[8] they support, who work for the Exchequer[9]. It is their job to make sure that everyone pays the duty – the tax on some of the cargo that comes in by sea. They are about as welcome here as an eel down a trouser-leg, especially as most of them are bullies and

---

5   Mining began in Cornwall in the Bronze Age and reached its height in the nineteenth century.
6   Mythical creatures, either pixie-like or souls of dead miners, heard knocking in other parts of the mine. Miners would often leave a small part of their pasty 'for the knockers'. A Cornish pasty was – and is – cooked meat and vegetables in a folded pastry case. (Once they may have been savoury at one end and sweet at the other, for a complete meal down the tin mine.)
7   Soldiers, who wore bright red uniforms. The whole idea of a uniform back then was to BE SEEN, not to act as camouflage.
8   The excise men were in charge of 'customs and excise' – the taxes and tariffs people had to pay when importing certain goods.
9   The Government's funds.

thieves and keep for themselves some of what they supposedly 'rescue' for the Crown.

My Uncle Jonah explains it this way:

"What should happen to, say, brandy, when it's brought into the country is that the price of the brandy and the price of transporting should be added together and then a little added on top for the man who sells it, to earn his living."

No one can argue with that. That's only fair!

"But no. Rich men and governments like to tax happiness to make it harder for poor men to be as happy as they are. So items which makes people happy, such as that brandy or silks or sot-weed[10], aren't sold that way. No, the Government charges a duty – a tax – on top, when it comes into the country. So the Exchequer's purse gets fuller than a glutton's[11] corporation[12], at the expense of the working man."

My uncle's right. 'Tis a proper disgrace, especially when duty is even charged on SALT[13], which we all need to eat to stay alive!

"These taxes are called customs and collected at the Customs Houses at the ports and harbours, but it's a most unfair custom if you ask me! And, to top it all, there's another tax called excises, collected to pay towards some war or other, long forgot or yet to come!

---

10   Eighteenth century slang for tobacco. You'll find Kitty uses a LOT of slang in this diary!

11   Greedy eater.

12   Big, fat tummy.

13   The word salary comes from the Latin word for salt, because Roman soldiers received some of their pay in salt, it was so vital.

"Now, this don't seem fair and proper to some folk, so they try to sneak in such cargo under the noses of the greedy excisemen without them being aware. This way, the poorer folk get to enjoy their pleasures a little cheaper, see? And this is why such folk call themselves free-traders, but the excisemen don't see it that way. They think of them as common criminals and call 'em smugglers. But condiddling[14] it ain't!"

Uncle Jonah speaks the truth! It's all very well for them stiff-rumps[15], with their high-paid positions and fancy clothes. But what about us? Well, as for me, I'm proud to say I'm a smuggler's daughter.

By that, I mean my father is a smuggler. My mother was a lady – some might have called her a blue-stocking[16] – a true and proper lady from a grand family in a grand home, and she taught me the reading and the writing, which few can do in Minnock, 'cept Squire Treppen, the priest, and a handful of officials with self-

14 Stealing (More eighteenth century slang!).
15 Haughty, stuck-up folk.
16 A knowledgeable woman.

important titles, strutting around like birds who've had their fill of seed. Since she died, me and my sister Esme have been mothered by Eliza, my brother being grown[17]. Some see Eliza simply as a cinder-garbler[18] but she's acted as everything from housekeeper to friend. But don't get me wrong. She's not all sweetness and light. I once saw her take a belt to her own boy – also a grown man now – and give him a right clapper-clawing.[19]

---

17   A grown man: a grown-up.
18   A female servant.
19   Thrashing/beating.

My father's name is Jon without the 'h', as was his father's and his father's before him, all the way back to when Jonah was livin' in that whale[20], or so my namesake uncle Jonah would have it. And by day, that is all that others call him. (No one ever calls my Uncle Jonah 'Jon' for short, for that would be far too confusing!)

By night, however, the villagers go by different names and, in all my short life, I have never heard them mix the two. My father's name by night is 'Captain', which shows just where he sits in the order of things: he's the one to give the orders and none give them to he. He carriers a pair of poppers[21], one on each hip, tucked inside his belt, all hid beneath that great long coat of his.

My Uncle Jonah is 'Patch', and our nearest neighbour, Robert Treggan, 'Goose'. The reasons for these names are less clear to me, but the reason for giving them is obvious:

---

20   A story from the Old Testament of the Bible.
21   Flintlock pistols.

should a redcoat or exciseman hear them calling out to each other in the dark, when they are about their less lawful pursuits, their identities will not be revealed!

Day 22

Just got back
from my uncle's
cottage over
by Hangman's
Cove. There'd
be no point in
bringing in cargo
to Minnock itself,
where Mr Duggan,
the exciseman with
his offices on the
harbour over at Fowle,
can walk right down
to the water's edge and
position his soldiers along the
shoreline. No, my father and his
companions need to bring in the
tax-free, duty-free, excise-free goods
into a cove, surrounded by craggy cliffs near
impossible to climb down. And which any
greedy, snooping exciseman imagines to be too

steep and difficult for smugglers to climb up. Little do they know! They are as much in the dark as a blindfolded mole![22]

There is a cave down on the beach of Hangman's Cove, its entrance well-hid by boulders, which has a passageway through the rocks which leads up to the clifftop, by which the smugglers come and go. This be ideal for moving contraband[23] by moonlight!

---

22 Moles aren't completely blind, of course, just very short-sighted.
23 Goods imported or exported illegally, without the payment of taxes.

This is very different to Cawsand[24], where I hear there are fifty free-trader boats taking regular trips to and from the Continent, as bold as brass and as bright as day!

Today, however, there was nothing to see but a few seals.[25] Come breeding-time, they'll rest up on the beach but today, with winter come, I only glimpsed a few out at sea; their bobbing smooth-grey heads like floating cannonballs. But they looked at me and I looked at them and we each knew that this is where we all belong.

24 Cawsand was the regular haunt of well-known smuggler Harry Carter. Customs services reckoned that, in 1804 alone, over 17,000 kegs of spirit were landed there. That's an average of over 46 kegs a DAY!
25 Grey seals, dolphins, basking sharks and even minke whales can all be seen on certain parts of the Cornish coast.

Day 28

Hangman's Cove got its name not from actual gallows where men were hanged. My father says in *his* grandfather's day, there were two stone arches jutting out into the water, formed naturally by waves wearing away rock over thousands of years. They've long since crumbled and been washed away, leaving nothing but two stone pillars we calls the Stacks.[26] But those arches reminded men of gallows and the hangman, and the name remains.

Some folk still like attending a good hanging[27]. It's a day out and chance to show and cheer and wave your fist, or clap and cheer and dance a jig, depending on who it is who's dangling, of course. But I don't like 'em when

---

26 Such geological arches, or their remains, can be found along the coast in the West Country, and the correct term for the remaining pillar of a fallen arch is actually a stack. One of the most famous arches is Durdle Dor in Dorset, near Lulworth Cove.

27 Hanging was a public spectacle in England until the Capital Punishment Amendment Act of 1868, after which they took place in prisons, in private.

it's one of our own, and steers well clear even if the others go to show support. Some men call hanging 'going up the ladder to sleep' to make it sound less dreadful. Perhaps they're the ones who may be afeared that they'll one day end up on the end of a rope themselves.

Uncle Jonah makes light of it, saying we all end up in an eternity box,[28] one way or another, and become the diet of worms! But I hope I die in my sleep aged 130, surrounded by my family[29]… not that I ever plan to marry and lose it all.[30]

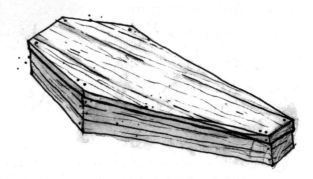

---

28   Coffin.
29   Life expectancy was far shorter than today. A poor person might be expected to die well before the age of forty.
30   When a woman married in the eighteenth century, she virtually became the property of her husband, losing individual rights, and all that had been hers became his.

But there are some things we do at Minnock of which I'm NOT so proud, and last night was one of them.

The wind was up and the windows rattled in their frames like my old Gran's teeth. The gate to our scrawny patch of garden at the front banged on its broken hinge and destroyed all chance of sleep. The candle guttered by my bed then was snuffed out as if by an invisible thumb and finger.[31] Tufts of marram grass[32], that thick and scrawny grass that seems to thrive in the salt air, waved like anemones beneath the waves pulled by

---

31 Wetting a thumb and forefinger and using it to 'pinch out' the flame on the wick was considered less messy than blowing it out. (Not recommended! Don't try it!) Richer folk had candle-snuffers for snuffing out – depriving the flame of oxygen – but not until the nineteenth century.

32 In the late eighteenth century, it was discovered that, if planted in sand dunes, marram grass would catch sand in its leaves, and its roots would grow down and bind the sand, stopping the dunes being washed away and, therefore, stabilising the coastline. The grass was then deliberately planted all over the world for just such a reason.

tidal waters. Then came the rain, lashing like the preacher's righteous tongue. (When the Reverend Glass gets preaching, even St Peter and St Andrew[33] – the saints in the stained-glass window – look guilty!)

When the wind began howling, Sovereign began howling too. He's a scrawny mutt but the best. He's grey with black and white blotches or white with grey and black blotches. (Uncle Jonah and I cannot agree.) My dad won't have a dog because the last thing he needs is a yelp or a bark to giveaway his whereabouts when moonraking.

Moonraking is another name for free-trading, and gets its name from one of the ways we've fooled those foolish excisemen over the years.

The story goes that there were a group of free-traders who hid their casks of smuggled brandy in the local village pond, dug deep to accommodate this hidden booty[34]. They did

---

33 The patron saints of fishermen.
34 No, not small boots, but valuable stolen goods or, in this case, illegally imported goods on which taxes were owed!

this at night, of course, to try to keep away from prying eyes. One night, however, when one of their number was pushing the final cask beneath the surface, an exciseman appeared like the Devil[35], as if from nowhere, and demanded to know what he was at[36].

---

35 The Devil appears regularly in Cornish myths and legends. In one, he is carrying a huge stone across the sky, to use to block the entrance to Hell. He is attacked by St Michael and the stone falls to the ground in a place then named Hell's Stone - later Helston – as a result, where it's said to have been built into the wall of The Angel Hotel!

36 What he was doing.

The exciseman was a right surly-boots[37]who had little time for tilly-tally,[38] so the smuggler knew that he must think quick! Seeing the full moon reflected in the pond and aware of the pole in his hand, he spoke as though he were a mopus.[39]

He gave a toothy grin and tried to look as best he could like a village idiot[40] of old.

"I is tryin' to catch that great silver coin, master," he said, stabbing at the Moon's round disk reflected on the water's surface, causing it to turn to ripples, "but it's 'arder than it looks."

The exciseman laughed at the fool. "You're trying to rake the moon, you hanktelo[41]!" he roared. "Away with you!" and kicked him up the behind.

But it was the exciseman himself who'd

---

37 Grumpy person. Yes, more eighteenth century slang, and there's plenty more to come.
38 Nonsense.
39 Simpleton/idiot.
40 Village idiots used to be a regular sight in villages across the country. A person of low ability, they may have been mocked and teased in their role, but were also well looked after.
41 Fool.

been hoodwinked.[42] The brandy was under his money-seeking nose without his even knowing it! And the name moonraker stuck.

---

42   Fooled/Had the wool pulled over his eyes/tricked.

My father needs to be able to slip in and out, hither and thither, as silently as a knife can gut a fish, and just as quick. Sovereign would be nothing but a hindrance at his side. When first he came to us, the pup was called Mutt. He is neither one breed nor the other but, on first meeting him, my Uncle Jonah picked him up and looked him square in the eye, declaring him to be one hundred percent Cornish. When I asked him how he could be so sure, he pronounced that it should be obvious to anyone who knows anything about dogs.

"You can tell a dog's intelligence by looking it in the eye," he said, "and Mutt, here, is a very intelligent dog indeed."

"So he must be Cornish?"

"That he must," my uncle nodded.

And he proved his intelligence and acquired his name[43] when he made a precious find: a

---

43   A sovereign was a gold coin, and a valuable one at that.

gold sovereign[44] mixed amidst the flotsam and jetsam[45] on the shore.

"Only a Cornish dog could find you such a treasure," Uncle Jonah declared. He reckons it was from a Spanish galleon[46] or a pirate ship, but I'm not some little girl fool enough to believe such childish tales. And surely Spanish coinage is gold doubloons? But Mutt was a much praised dog that day, and Sovereign he became.

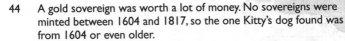

---

44 A gold sovereign was worth a lot of money. No sovereigns were minted between 1604 and 1817, so the one Kitty's dog found was from 1604 or even older.

45 Bits and bobs washed ashore and deposited on the beach.

46 Vessel.

There was no full moon last night as he howled along with the wind, the gate banged, the windows rattled, the rain lashed down, and my candle guttered. Then I heard the cries and, leaping from my bed and running to the window, I saw a cluster of men hurrying to our cottage, lanterns waving. The old navy man Jack Treviss was easy to spot amongst them, what with his being a go dot and carry![47] He had trouble keeping up with them, though, his peg-leg slowing him down.

---

47 'A go dot and carry' is eighteenth century slang for someone with a wooden leg. He goes (moves his wooden leg), lands it, leaving a dot, and then carries it (lifts it) to land it again, leaving another dot.

I sat at the
top of the stairs
and watched
my big brother, Jago,
open the door to Tom Tregowan,
a man who looks slipperier than an eel at the
best of times but was now soaked to the skin
and gleaming by lamplight. His night-name
be Flint.

"We're here to see the Captain," he said,
"There's a ship in trouble out by Cannon's

Point." His crooked teeth reminded me of the gravestones in our tiny cliff-top churchyard.

"The Captain's not here," said Jago. He's a full-grown man and a handsome one at that, with a few day's growth of stubble on that square jaw of his. "Do you know the ship?"

"It's too difficult to identify in this weather. We can't make out no name."

"Its colours?" asked my brother.[48]

"French," said Flint.

"You're sure?"

"As days.[49] Despite this weather so foul, I could make it out clear with the glass[50]."

"How low in the water?" asked Jago, for as to how low a vessel sat was an indication of how heavy it was, and whether it was laden with cargo or returning home empty.

"Low," said Flint.

There were mutterings of agreement from those behind him. "Mighty low."

---

48 He was asking what country's flag the ship was flying.
49 As sure as night will follow day. In other words, a certainty.
50 Spyglass was a common name for a telescope, and glass was an abbreviation of that.

"Do you think it might be one of our friends from the continent?" asked Jago. He meant those helping with the smuggling from Europe.

"We need to speak with your father –" repeated Tom Tregowan.

"Like I said, he's not here," said Jago. There was a certain menace in his voice, as though he was daring these older men to stand up to him. My brother can be quite a bully. I should know. When we were younger, he would frighten me with tales of standing stones[51], or twist my arm to make my skin burn. "What would you ask him if he were here?" he demanded. "Do you want to know if we should light a beacon on the headland to warn them off the rocks?"

"Too late for that," said Jack Treviss, the old seaman with the wooden leg, still panting to catch his breath.

"Then what?" said Jago.

Sovereign, who had been sitting by the fire,

---

51   There are many standing stones in Cornwall, erected by pre-historic people, their purpose lost in the mists of time. Many myths grew up about them, such as the one about a group of stones, called the Hurlers, on Bodmin Moor. These were said to be people turned to stone for playing games on a Sunday, the Lord's day.

came over to see what all the excitement was about, sniffing at the men's feet. Jago put his boot under the dog and flipped him out of the way. It wasn't exactly a kick, but it took all of my strength not to run downstairs and kick HIM. But that would give away my presence, so I bit my lip and stayed where I was on the stairs.

"What to do, Jago," said Jack Treviss. "We came to ask the captain what to do."

"It's just that if these Frenchmen *ain't* no friends of ours…" said another man.

"And they're weighed down with cargo…" added yet another.

"We're all men of the sea," said Jago. "I say we rescue them, but quietly, like, so as not to attract attention… and if we was to rescue their cargo too and were to look after it as if it were our own, then all the better!" He grinned a handsome grin and no one misunderstood his meaning. "I say we get down there at once. All this talk and the ship could already be stranded and its cargo waiting to be claimed!"

Grabbing his coat from a hook by the open door, he ducked outside to join the men. "What are you waiting for?" he bellowed in the wind. I saw him being handed a lantern before the door was closed behind him.

I felt my heart beat faster and a tingle of excitement reached my fingers. I knew what this meant. Tonight, the men of Minnock would not be smugglers, but wreckers![52]

Back in my room, by the light through the open door from the fire dying in the grate below, I pulled on my clothes over my tattered nightshirt and hurried back down the stairs. I patted and praised Sovereign, made him sit, and I reached for one of the storm lanterns hanging from a beam and lit it with a taper[53] from the fire. Reaching up and wrapping one of my father's scarves around me, I went out into the night, to follow at a distance. Jack Treviss, swinging his wooden leg in his stride, was at the rear.

I was almost bowled over by the wind, it was so strong. No wonder the Frenchmen's vessel was against the rocks! Sovereign's howls from the house were snatched away the instant the

---

52   There is much misunderstanding and myth about wreckers. Over the years the term has come to mean people who deliberately lured ships onto rocks, sometimes by lighting fires inland, tricking sailors into thinking they were warning beacons at the land's edge, so they brought their vessels in too close to the shore where they were wrecked. This may have happened but was VERY rare. Wreckers were people who plundered the cargo from wrecked ships as soon as possible, often before the crew had been rescued or had the chance to escape.

53   A long, thin piece of paper which, once alight, was used to light lamps and stoves.

wind whipped around my head. I followed the only path my father and his men could have taken.

I reached Cannon's Point and watched as a small procession of lanterns made their way down the treacherous cliff path, bobbing like glowing insects, to the beach below.

I would not venture by that route even on the brightest summer's day. On a dark and stormy winter's night such as last night was, it would have been madness, and as foolish as signing one's own death warrant[54] or arm-wrestling with an octopus. Jago and my father's men were used to such conditions and sure-footed as mountain goats. Even Jack Treviss, the one-legged man, followed, slow but sure. Father forbade him from entering the cave at Hangman's Cove, for fear of slowing the line when taking cargo in and out but, for a man with but one leg, he was steady and confident.

I took the longer, safer, route but – from the terrible crashing of wood and cries of men, the likes of which I have never heard before – I knew that the wind and raging sea had brought a vessel onto the treacherous rocks. When I finally reached the shore, the wind had dropped considerably and the rain become a mere drizzle…

---

54 An official document authorising that someone may be taken dead or alive.

…but nothing prepared me for the sight that awaited me. Jago had already divided the men into two parties: those trying to rescue the men and those salvaging the cargo. All was undertaken by the lights of the lanterns and a few hastily-lit fires. Jago's attention was directed towards the cargo spilling from the wreck of the French vessel: crates and barrels, some bobbing in the sea, some smashed and useless on the needle-like rocks and some already ashore.

Our Minnock men were roped together for safety: two human chains, one for guiding rescued sailors from man to man to shore, the other for passing cargo from vessel to beach. Just because the weather was the Frenchie's enemy didn't make it the Cornishman's friend and, when it came to the cargo, my brother's intensions were obvious and threefold: to gain as much booty as possible, as quickly as possible, as safely as possible.

He was far too busy in the dark and noise and mayhem to notice me crouched behind a boulder at a safe distance. But, when dawn broke, I knew it was time to return home before he did. The wind and rain had dropped to nothing, and much of the cargo was already claimed and being carted off to be hid.

Shocked and injured Frenchie sailors were huddled together in groups, tending to each other's wounds, tearing clothes to make strips of bandage; using splintered pieces of their own wrecked vessel to make splints.

I was jerrymumbling[55] as I ran, not just from the wet and the wind but through the shock of what I'd seen. By the time I reached the cottage, I felt somewhat downhearted. I have always seen the people of Minnock as heroes,

---

55 Shaking.

with my father at their head. They are free-traders, fighting an unjust system and red-coats who are in it as much for their own. But seeing those poor injured sailors filled me with sadness. Yes, my father's gang rescued them, under Jago's guidance, but might they have saved *more* of them had not the cargo also been on their mind?

Day 29

All talk around the village is of the ship that was somehow blown ashore and wrecked upon the rocks. There are a goodly number of survivors, with the injured tended by our local doctor, Dr Treloon, and by the Reverend Glass. The others have been housed in the one place big enough to hold them: Hanson's Boatshed.

It has been agreed that the dead be buried here in a communal grave[56] and that, at some future date, a memorial stone will be erected, though I have my doubts. There was remarkably little cargo to be salvaged in the light of day, though Ma Truttock did manage to find a barrel of port and became so glorious[57] that she fell face down into the sand, or so the gossip goes. I have seen others reeling

---

56   One large grave rather than separate graves being dug. It was the law of the sea that where bodies were washed up, locals would bury them. This would be reassuring for those who lost their own fathers, sons or brothers at sea, hoping the same was true for them.

57   Ecstatically drunk.

about the village today, as full as a goat,[58] as though dancing to a silent tune, and take it that a few other such casks have washed ashore and been claimed and sampled in an instant.

I made my way up to Cannon's Point to look down upon the scene and came face to face with Mr Duggan.

Mr Duggan is the chief exciseman in these parts, based in a harbour-side office, near the Customs House, in the nearby town of Fowle. A barrel of a man – more muscle than fat – he has little need for a neck, so his head seems to join his body without one, leaving just enough

---

58   Drunk.

room for a jet-black neckerchief, looking
not unlike a dead bat! He has a fearful scar
running vertically above and below his right
eye, though the eye itself – a piercing blue – is
undamaged. There are many rumours as to
how he got such an injury, the most popular

being "poking his head in where it did not belong." I would not say my father is afraid of him, but it is a foolish man, woman or child who is not, at the very least, wary of the chief exciseman.

Uncle Jonah says that Mr Duggan is no oaf. He has a sharp mind to go with his bull-beef[59] looks, which is why he should be doubly feared. He's not like other excisemen who spend their time counting waves[60] or making a great harvest out of little corn[61]. Duggan don't just look. He *sees*.

Flanked by two redcoats, Mr Duggan was standing ahead of me, studying the ground, prodding at it in placing with his walking cane. He saw me from the corner of his eye. "Here, you, girl!" he commanded. "What is your name?"

"Kitty Cask, sir," I replied without hesitation. I know it's best not to lie when you don't have to and, that way, you can't be caught out by it.

---

59 Big and grim.
60 Wasting time.
61 Making a big fuss out of nothing.

"Jon Cask's girl? Well, what are you doing here, young Kitty Cask? Come to spy?"

"No, sir," I said. "I've come to look down upon the wreck. It be the talk of the village."

"You're too late, girl," said Mr Duggan. "The wind and sea has done its worst. You'll see nothing more than floating planks, which I hardly think will raise the blood[62]."

"I see, sir," I said and turned to leave. "Thank you, sir."

"If it was bodies you were hoping to see, save that for the hanging."

I stopped in my tracks, my feet upon the bouncy cliff-top turf.

---

62   Get you excited.

I turned back to face the ghastly Mr Duggan. "Hanging, sir?"

"When I catch the men who stripped the vessel of all its pickings as the Jimmy Rounds floundered all around 'em," he said.

(Jimmy Rounds is what many men call Frenchies, on account of it sounding like *Je me rends*, which is what most Frenchies say if they face an Englishmen – and certainly a Cornishman – in a fight, for it means "I surrender!")

A gull screeched above me. Then another.

"I don't know what you mean, sir," said I.

The exciseman's eyes met mine. "I'm *sure* you don't, Miss Kitty Cask," he said, "but that cargo should have been collected by my men and made safe under lock and key.

Theft is theft and custom and excise duties are there to be paid." He then turned his back on me and strode towards the headland.

My father and his fellow smugglers laugh at how they run rings around Mr Duggan. I hear them talking sometimes when they think I am abed. But they know to watch out for Mr Duggan, for he is like a sleeping jellyfish. Get too close and he stings.[63]

Arriving back home, I found Eliza cooking fish stew upon the range[64].

"Where's thy been, Kit?" she asked. She always calls me Kit, as though I am a boy (for Kit is short for Christopher, like the saint).

"For a walk," I told her.

"An' you steered clear o' the wreck as I bade[65] you?"

---

63   For most people, the sting from the average jellyfish is no worse than a nettle sting: unpleasant but more irritating than painful. But there is a particular type of jellyfish called the Portuguese Man of War which has a very nasty sting, and can be found off Cornish waters and washed up on Cornish beaches. And are best left WELL ALONE!

64   A large iron cooker, heated with coal or – as in this instance – wood.

65   Bid you/asked you to.

"Yes," I said, for it were true. "I saw Mr Duggan, though."

"Did he see you?"

"Yes, as if anyone could avoid his eye," I said. I meant by day, of course, because by night my father keeps well beyond his sight!

"And what were you about, Kit?" she asked, her eyes fixed on mine.

"Like I said, I were walking."

She smiled her smile. "You always know more than you're letting on," she said, "but I never knows how much that be!"

I laughed.

At that moment, my father came into the house, my little sister Esme upon his shoulders, meaning that he had to bend his knees and she duck her head to fit beneath the lintel[66]. He must have returned this morning when I was about my walk.

"Ah, Kitty!" he boomed when his eyes fell upon me. "I has a job for you!"

"What is it?" I asked, excitedly.

"I need you to go to the gospel-shop and give the old glue-pot a message," he said.

Eliza looked outraged and banged her spoon on the side of her cooking pot, exclaiming, "Jon Cask, you'll burn in Hell if you talk in such a manner!", for though 'gospel-shop' is harmless enough a word or two for a church, I'm not sure the Reverend Glass would take

---

66   Top of the door frame.

too kindly to being called a glue-pot[67] – old or otherwise – despite it not being personal but the slang for any parson[68]!

My father gave a cheeky grin and covered his mouth as though he were a naughty child.

Eliza tried to hide her grin and over-concentrated on stirring the fish stew some more.

I found the Reverend Glass in the church, looking far from happy.

"Hello, Kitty," he said. "A sad day, what with those poor souls lost so close to shore and to safety."

"Not too many of 'em, though,

67 The nickname 'glue-pot' comes from *joining together* men and women in holy matrimony!

68 A member of the clergy, such as a priest or vicar.

Reverend," I said, thinking of our men roped together in the water, getting them to shore. "And they *was* Frenchmen," I reminded him.

"We are all equal in the eyes of God," he said, which I found confusing because I know we pray for victory against the enemy in times of war, but I said nothing.

"What about the Israelites?" piped up a squeaky voice I recognised at once, and from out behind the pulpit stepped Master James Treppen. You have never seen a boy so clean – a *person* so clean – and everything about him, from his hair to his skin to his nails, looks scrubbed and buffed to a shine. And his clothes? They are cut from a very different cloth to mine!

"The Israelites?" asked Reverend Glass.

"You say that we are all equal in the eyes of God, but aren't the Israelites God's chosen people?"

"Our Lord did come from the Holy Land[69]," the vicar said with a nod as though it were an answer. "What brings you here, Kitty?"

"I have a message from my father," I said, holding out a folded piece of paper[70].

"What does it say?" squeaked Master James Treppen.

"Do you think I've been fed with a fire shovel?" I scowled.

He looked at me, his face a blank. I was forgetting that, as the son of the local squire who owns much of the land about these parts[71], he was not used to the sayings of us common folk!

---

69   Israel and Palestine. In the eleventh, twelfth, and thirteenth centuries, European Christians fought Crusades to try to win the city of Jerusalem from Muslims.

70   In eighteenth century England, paper was expensive, but not as expensive as parchment or vellum. Parchment was made from sheep or goat's skin and, even more expensive, vellum was mad from calf's skin. Paper was made from plant materials, generally linen taken from old rags, collected by the likes of a 'rag and bone man'.

71   Eighteenth century squires were powerful people. Legend has it that, in neighbouring Wales, a Squire Lloyd wanted to buy a farm that was spoiling the view from his house but the famer would not sell. So the squire reported his prize black ram missing, then had it lowered down the farmer's chimney and into the house, at night. He then brought the constable to the farmhouse and had the farmer arrested for theft. He was hanged and the farm became the squire's.

"What do you mean?" he said.

"For someone who knows all about the Israelites, I'm sure you can work it out, James," I said.

He gave me one of his looks. "You would need an exceptionally large mouth to be able to eat with a fire shovel," he reasoned, "so you mean that you're not a big mouth? You do not give away secrets?"

"Or private communications between my father and the Reverend," I said, with a nod. "See. It was not difficult, was it?"

The vicar laughed. He knew full well that this was no way for a fisherman's daughter to talk to the squire's son! But my mother had been a Treppen also – but, as a woman, would have inherited no land or money, even had she lived.

"Will you come with me down to the harbour, Kitty?" piped James.

"And why should I want to be seen with a young hemp[72] like you?" I teased.

---

72   Graceless boy.

"Because I have a sixpence to spend, Kitty Cask. That's why!"

"A bender[73]? Why didn't you say so?" I cried. "Let's go!" I nodded at the Reverend Glass. "Good day to you, Reverend," I said.

The Reverend smiled as he watched us go but, when I glanced back, I could see that he was already engrossed in my father's message.

With the church of St Andrew & St Peter at the

---

73   A bender – sixpence – was a lot of money for a boy to have. (Beer, for example, was less than a penny a pint.)

top of the hill and the harbour down by the
sea – for where else could it be? – it was quite
a distance. Young James Treppen took it upon
himself to run all the way and I wasn't going to
let him beat me!

I've not much else to report about the day other than later I saw a group of redcoats, themselves the worse for drink, surrounding Ivy Thomas outside the dairy, jeering and calling her names. Sometimes I wish I were me brother and would give them what for! As much as I hate Mr Duggan, I respect that he's trying to uphold the law, however wrong it be. But these men? They're soldiers to the King, policing these shores, but many are just in it for themselves, *using* the law to their own ends. My father says that their corruption makes them worse than honest smugglers! And who am I to argue?

Speaking of Mr Duggan, he passed me in his carriage[74] and, I'm sad to report, he had a most SATISFIED smile upon his face, as though he'd made good progress in his investigation. And anything good for the exciseman is bad for us.

---

74   By the end of the seventeenth/beginning of the eighteenth century, carriages had spring 'shock absorbers', stopping the passengers feeling every lump and bump and cart rut in the unmade-up roads, making journeys that much more comfortable.

Day 32

There are four ale houses in Minnock, but only one has two cellars: a secret one beside the ordinary cellar where the kegs of ale are stored. This is The Black Eye and, though the sign outside shows a sailor with a black eye-patch, the name is a pun – a play on words – for to give a bottle a black eye is to drain it empty… and there's plenty of that goes on within!

Sometimes, it is necessary to move some of the contraband about the village during daylight. This is safe enough, as long as it's not witnessed by those few well-to-do folk who do NOT watch the wall[75] when the gentlemen go by, and are likely to speak out of turn and tell the redcoats or the excisemen.

Our neighbour Robert Treggan had just removed a small cask of rum from the secret

---

75   People turning away as smugglers pass with their contraband so, if asked by the authorities, they can genuinely say that they saw nothing! In some villages, just about everyone was happy about smuggling because it meant cheaper goods for everyone!

cellar – where much of the smuggled goods are stored – and brought it up through the hatch into the bar, and was rolling it across the floor when there was a cry of "Reds!" and, seconds later, a swarm of redcoats came spilling through the door.

I was seated beneath a table, surrounded by legs and feet but still with a good view of the action. I'd been watching Robert Treggan roll the cask, turned to the door at the cry of

"Reds!" and turned back again, thinking our neighbour would be found out and carted off to jail… but the cask had disappeared.

One minute it had been there, the next moment nothing.

It had vanished into thin air.

The leader of the soldiers, that crab-lanthorn[76] Sergeant Byron, gave the order that none of us move, and a search was undertaken.

---

76   Irritable man.

"I've nothing to hide," roared the landlord, Jake Polgate, "and if your clumsy men break so much as a bottle you'll know all about it. Betty, keep an eye!"

The drinkers roared their approval.

Betty, the landlord's wife, is a tall woman with arms the size of hams. Holding a bottle of blue glass in one hand, she was standing next to Robert Treggan, towering above him. She folded her arms and glared at the soldiers.

"SILENCE!"

shouted Sergeant Byron, but we were having none of it.

Byron drew his sword. The sound of the blade against the scabbard is not a pleasant one. The room hushed. Like it or not, these were the King's men and their powers are great. And, of course, we DID have something to hide – that cask of rum – wherever it had gone!

I heard the redcoats go behind the bar and into the cellar but, with the entrance to the

other, secret, cellar well hid, they came up empty handed. They looked under tables but all they found was me. I was dragged out by my ear.

"What have we here?" said Byron.

"Leave her alone!" someone shouted.

"What were you doing under there?" demanded the sergeant.

"Sitting," I said.

"What do you think she were doing?" demanded Betty Polgate. "She's too big to *stand* beneath a table, ain't she?"

There were more roars of laughter.

Mr Duggan ducked through the doorway and entered The Black Eye now. The room fell silent. He looked me up and down.

"Ah, young Kitty Cask," he said. "We meet again." He turned to Sergeant Byron. "Anything?" he asked.

"Nothing, sir," said the redcoat.

"Then we're leaving," said Mr Duggan. And they did.

It was a good few minutes after the exciseman and the redcoats had gone that the coast was declared clear. And it was then I discovered how that little cask of rum had been magicked away…

Betty Polgate lifted her skirt and petty coats and there it was beneath them! The drinkers roared their approval and raised their tankards as Robert Treggan gave her an exaggerated bow.

"Why, thankee lady!" he said, as she sat down on the barrel with a laugh.

I certainly had a story to tell my father when I got back home.

Day 33

I overheard something today and, though glad that I did so – so that I could pass on a warning – my heart sank at the news. Today has been one of those crisp, cold, days filled with sunshine that makes you glad to be alive. I was lying in my father's boat, staring up at the sky, watching the birds wheel above me. I've heard people call them seagulls as if there were such a bird[77]! What I saw were blacked-headed gulls, common gulls and terns. All different, all scavengers and, like the rest of us in Minnock, living off the sea.

---

77   A seagull isn't a type of bird like, say, a robin
or a sparrow is. It's a general term for different types of gull
that live near the sea.

I must have drifted off to sleep but, when I awoke, I heard two men talking as they passed me by. (The boat was pulled up onto the beach, above the high tide mark, and I was high enough up to be hidden from view.)

I recognised both voices instantly, though they spoke in lowered tones. These were Mr Duggan and Sergeant Byron!

"You're sure the information is good this time?" asked Mr Duggan.

"It was good last time, sir," said Byron. "It's just that Mrs Polgate was too clever by half with her dress."

"She won't be able to play that trick a second time," said Mr Duggan, "whatever she may think."

"We have them now," said Byron. "It's only a matter of time."

I shuddered. It was likely the sergeant could only have known about the landlady's trick with the dress if someone who had been there had told him later. And, from what Byron had said, someone – probably that same someone – had suggested that he raid The Black Eye in the first instance, for he would find the contraband being moved!

After enough time had passed for me to be sure that the redcoat and the exciseman were long gone, I slipped out of the boat, jumped

down to the ground, hurried
up the shore and began
to run homeward.

I had to warn Father
that there is a
spy in our midst!

Eliza was out when I arrived back home and
little Esme was having a nap. I found Father
sitting and staring into the fire, the dancing
flame reflected in his eyes. I told him of what
I had heard.

He sucked upon his pipe before he spoke; a long-stemmed clay affair[78]. "Good girl!" he said, at last. "We can learn much from that conversation."

"That there's a viper in the nest!" said I.

Father nodded his head slowly. I don't think he was ever as handsome a man as my brother, Jago, but he has kinder eyes. Far kinder eyes. "If that Sergeant Byron had just been talking of Betty's hiding of the cask beneath her frills, it could simply have been overheard gossip from some brandy-face.[79] It might even have been second-hand news, spoken by someone who'd heard it from someone else who'd been there."

I nodded again.

"But the fact that the red said that he had

---

78   Ever since Sir Walter Raleigh brought tobacco back to England from the Americas in the late sixteenth century, clay pipes were popular. In the seventeenth century, there were a huge number of clay-pipe smokers. In the 18th century, they declined in number – especially with the ever-rising tax on tobacco -- and it became more fashionable for the upper classes to take snuff. The longer the stem, the cooler the smoke and the greater the likelihood the stem would break.

79   Drunkard.

raided the ale house on account of having information means that one of our number has been talking… but not one of those closest to me. Not one who knows all."

"How so?" I asked.

"Because whoever told Sergeant Byron of the moving of some cargo did not know of the secret cellar, which would have been the greatest prize!"

Of course! I wished that I'd thought of that. It seemed so obvious, now that my father had said it. The secret entrance to the secret cellar remained hidden. That had not been given away.

"And, thanks to the quick thinking of Betty Polegate, the original information turned out to be three skips of a louse![80]" he added.

"So what will you do?" I asked.

"From what you overheard, my clever Kitty, this informant has given Byron and Duggan more information, though we don't yet know what."

---

80   Worth little or nothing.

"Be careful, Father!" I urged. "Whoever it is may have revealed you to be 'Captain'."

He pulled his pipe from his mouth and grinned. "I'm always careful," he said, "and, if he has told them I'm Captain, why haven't they come to arrest me? Because they know they need *proof* first, and will have to catch me with the contraband! What's more, this fellow – whoever he may be – could turn out to be little more than water in my shoe."[81] Then his face suddenly became serious. "Kitty –" he began.

---

81   Annoying.

"Yes?"

"That wreck the other night. I know you'll have heard talk of all the booty claimed… of all that cargo taken –" he paused to find the right words "– but know that Jago and the men saved many a life that night too, Frenchman or not."

I could not tell Father of what I'd seen down on the beach, for that would have meant my telling him I had been there.

"I might have done things differently. I cannot say for sure, for I was in Fowle and it was your brother who had to make decisions, on the spur of the moment in the heart of a storm… Do not be angry with him, Kitty."

"I'm not angry with Jago," I lied.

My father snorted at the comment, tobacco smoke coming from his nostrils like a dragon's. *"Not angry with Jago?* Why, if the looks you gave him were daggers, he'd have been stabbed a thousand times!" He grinned again. "You're like your dear, departed mother. She was always quick to take the owl."[82]

I like it when Father compares me to Mother, though I've never been clear as to why anger should be likened to owl-snatching. Though, I suppose, a snatched owl would be far from happy!

---

82   "Take the owl" means to 'get angry', though the origins of the phrase are unclear. Owls give out a terrible screech when hunting which could, perhaps, be compared with a screech of rage.

Day 34

I write this with a shaking hand, for events have taken a terrible turn tonight. Father, in the guise of Captain, was supervising the unloading of some free-trade booty in Hangman's Cove when disaster struck. Redcoats seemed to appear out of nowhere!

I suppose I should say that although my father has never made secret from me the fact that he's a smuggler, he has always forbidden my being there when the goods are brought ashore.

"It's dangerous enough to be caught with it stashed and stowed away," he once told me, "but on the beach at night there's the darkness, sea, rolling barrels and crates to contend with, quite apart from the dangers of the excisemen. It's no place for you, no matter how bold and brave you be."

And, in return, I've never told him that I've become very good at creeping out of the house at night, undetected by Eliza, and following them!

This evening, in the guise of Captain, he gave his men extra instruction. He didn't tell them that he had fears of a spy somewhere along the line, but he did give orders that they be 'extra careful' and he posted extra lookouts on the cliffs.

The excisemen often post lookouts of their own. We call 'em watchers or watchmen. More times than not, they might be encouraged to take a drink or two or, those less willing, might find themselves with a sack over their head and trussed like a chicken for a night on the heather before being discovered next day! It's harder when there are groups of them or an eager watchman rides back and forth across the clifftops on horseback, eyes peeled for any sign of smugglers at work.

Satisfied that they were unseen, my father then led his men down through the secret passage and out of the hidden cave mouth onto the beach. I crouched and followed them before the lookouts were even in place, watching for redcoats.

It was a dark night and the vessel my father and the men of Minnock were waiting for was painted black. I knew its name to be *The Selkie*,[83] but this too was painted out. Even though we knew that it was out there, I found it impossible to see.

Uncle Jonah had said that much of the success of the freetrader is down to advance planning. You need:

• A specified cargo (so you don't end up with crates of lace when you're planning a celebration needing plenty of brandy).

---

83   There are a number of Cornish myths about selkies; seals who can take on human form and live amongst people – forced to stay that way if people hide their skin – but, once in their skin, they become seals once more and go back to the sea.

- The ship carrying the cargo to be at the agreed place at the agreed time (so that everyone is in position, ready and waiting).

- The ship to be as camouflaged/hidden as possible (because prevention men[84] are everywhere).

- To take precautions to avoid the prevention men (which is nothing but the best common sense).

- Enough men, horses and wagons to carry the cargo (because you certainly don't want to have to leave some behind).

- Somewhere big enough and safe enough to store the cargo, once ashore[85].

Hiding the cargo in the cave at Hangman's

---

84 Customs men, excisemen, constables and soldiers. In other words, just about anyone out to prevent (stop) the smuggling.
85 There are even instances of church crypts being used to store smuggled goods, in full knowledge of the clergyman!

Cove, where the loot itself comes ashore, saves a lot of manpower. No need for endless horses or carts to carry it off into the night, increasing the chance of being caught, red-handed.[86]

In order to let the smugglers know that the ship was out there, one of its crew fired a barrel-less pistol with gunpowder in the pan, creating a flash of blue light, without the loud BANG.[87]

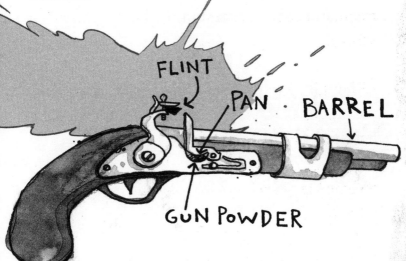

FLINT

PAN

BARREL

GUN POWDER

---

86 The phrase 'caught red-handed' dates back to the fifteenth century, and the red probably refers to the blood of a murder victim, or to the blood of a poached animal.

87 The phrase 'a flash in the pan', referring to a brief success that's not followed up, comes from flintlock pistols. If there's a flash in the pan, it's not followed up with the successful firing of shot.

'Goose' – our neighbour Robert Treggan – fired a responding flash to show the coast was clear.[88] It was time for action. In next to no time, rowing boats were coming into view, laden with goodies.[89]

But then the best-laid plan went well awry. As the cargo of tea, lace, whiskey, and baccy was rowed ashore, the redcoats appeared – not from the clifftops *but from the cave itself*, where they had been lying in wait.

WE HAD BEEN BETRAYED!

---

88 In this case, the coast was literally – or seemingly – clear of unwanted guests: the redcoats. The phrase, however, has come to mean that it's safe to proceed because there's no one watching or listening.

89 The rather modern-sounding word 'goody' dates back to 1754 and refers to something tasty! 1765 saw the publication of a nursery tale called The History of Little Goody Two-Shoes, about a girl who had one shoe… until the end!

It was Tom Tregowan who gave the warning shout and, so that others were left in no doubt that there was trouble, my father fired a flintlock in the air. What happened next was pandemonium. Some redcoats fired their rifles and, while they reloaded, others fired, then others.

The smugglers threw themselves behind the nearest rock or crate or barrel. The few of them with pistols returned fire. I saw Tom

Tregowan draw a dagger from his boot and one giant of a man – a farmer by the name of Garton – lifted a barrel and threw it in front of a group of advancing soldiers. It bounced as it hit the sand, without breaking, and rolled into the men like a ball into skittles,[90] the soldiers scattering or falling.

---

90   West Country skittles was a popular pastime behind inns/ale houses/pubs. They are still played today, and a number of pubs – especially in Somerset and Dorset – have rooms containing skittle alleys.

There was chaos, with arm to arm fighting, shouting, grunts and cries. Rowing boats, weighed down with illegal cargo, were being rowed frantically away from the action.

The darkness was both an advantage and disadvantage: I couldn't clearly see the enemy but they couldn't clearly see me. I couldn't tell friend from foe, but neither could they. A shot from a redcoat's rifle would give away his position, and one of ours might fire back, flinging themselves to one side so that, should the soldiers return fire, their target would be replaced by thin air.

Once fired, a rifle had to be reloaded down its muzzle[91], an action quite difficult in the dark… but it could very easily used as another kind of weapon. With a bayonet[92] fixed at the end, and held out in front of them, a redcoat's rifle became quite a spear: good for ripping open sacks when on the look-out for contraband; for prodding haystacks when in search of hiding men; or forcing smugglers to keep their distance in the dark on the beach at Hangman's Cove or, worse still, lancing them.

With surprise on their side – the informant

---

91   Barrel.
92   A blade fixed at the end of a rifle.

who'd told them of what to look for at The Black Eye must also have told them of the existence of the cave and where to find its hidden entrance – and with far more redcoats than ever seen in Minnock at one time, we were outmanoeuvred and outnumbered.

But, when my father cried, "Withdraw!" we did have one thing to our advantage. The freetraders know this cove by night better than any redcoat and they melted away into the darkness, except for two wounded. And my father.

One of these was Flint – Tom Tregowan – who'd been hit in the leg by rifle shot and was half-lying, half-sitting upon the sand, back propped against a rock, just ahead of me.

A redcoat started running towards him with his rifle out in front of him, bayonet fixed. I had to do something. But what? I fumbled for a stone and threw it wildly at the soldier, hitting him on the head. He turned around in rage and must have dimly made out my figure in the darkness.

As he ignored Tom Tregowan and charged at me, I slipped and fell, only to feel myself being scooped up in a large man's hand.

"Put–" I began, then felt another hand being clamped across my mouth.

"Sshh, Limpet," whispered a voice, and I recognised it at once as belonging to my father. A moment later, it was followed by his giving out a

shuddering cry as, I later realised, the bayonet caught his side from behind. But he did not drop me, and he ran.

"Captain! Are you all right?" cried Tom.

"Save yourself!" shouted my father.

Back home, I knew that I would have much explaining to do, but first things first, we needed to tend to my father's wound. Once a safe distance from the cove, he'd put me back down upon my own two feet and we had run abreast. By the time we neared the cottage, I was supporting him as he held his side.

Eliza tore a bed sheet into strips while I got a bowl of water and Sovereign licked my father's face, which may not have pleased him but was, at least, a distraction.

"You'll live," said Eliza when the wound was washed and dressed. "A tougher man might call it a mere scratch." From the amount of blood in the bowl and on the rags, I knew her to be teasing and he took it in good faith.

"And if you were a better nurse this scratch might not kill me!" he replied, with a grin.

Sitting quietly by the fire, a warm brandy in his belly, he now turned his attention to me. The moment I had been dreading.

"Do you think I don't know you follow me some nights?" he asked. "Who would be worthy to lead his men if he didn't spot his own daughter ducking behind a milestone here or a hedge there?"

"You knew?" I asked in genuine surprise.

"Of course I knew."

"Then why didn't you stop me?"

"I've told you many times of the dangers, Kitty," he said. "I've as much as ordered you never to risk your own life or others."

"Others?"

"Do you think I'd turn my back on a bayonet for anyone but you or your little sister? Do you think I'd have left Tom to fend for himself when I could have helped him?"

I burst into tears and flung my arms around him. Feeling him flinch in pain, I hurriedly let go. "Oh, father, I'm so sorry…"

"No time for snivelling, Kit," he said.

"But if you knew, why did you never confront me or shout at me or lock me in my room or beat me with a belt?"

My father laughed. "And if I had confronted you or shouted at you or locked you in a room or beaten you with a belt, would you still have followed us on our night time journeys?"

"Yes," I said without a moment's hesitation.

"Then there's your answer. You are your mother's daughter, fierce and independent. I can ask you to be wise and sensible, but I cannot make you, Kitty. You are who you are.

Half Cask and half Treppen. Now, away to bed with you."

Sovereign slept on my bed that night, but I could not sleep for fear that Tom Tregowan might have been run-through with a redcoat's bayonet. And it was my fault.

I must have finally drifted off, however, for I was awoken by the creak of my bedroom door opening. It was Jago!

"Father asked me to tell you that all is well," he said, in the shadow of my candle, still burning at my bedside.

"Tom Tregowan?" I asked, sitting upright.

"Not a single man left behind on the beach," he said. "A disappointing night for Duggan, I imagine!"

"But how?" I asked.

"I'm a one-man army, me," he said. "And strong enough to carry two wounded men without so much as breaking a sweat." I could hear the smile in his voice.

I pummelled his chest with my fists. "You're just a strutting peacock!" I said, giving him a hug. He smelt of saltwater, brandy and gunpowder. Then a thought occurred to me. "What of the lookouts? They must have been caught before being able to give warning."

"The detail of redcoats later marching them to jail were met by a mob," he said, "who *persuaded* them to let the men go. And I think you'll find our very own Eliza was amongst them! Now, don't waste any more of your candle, and go to sleep," said my brother.

I nodded but, when he'd gone, I slipped out of bed and – with a much happier heart – wrote this entry in my diary.

Day 36

Father and one other have been arrested!

The soldiers came at dawn and, though Sovereign gave warning, it was not soon enough. The front door, not locked, burst open, and a dozen redcoats spilled in. By the time I had jumped from my bed and begun running down the stairs, Father was already struggling under the weight of five or six soldiers, manhandling him to the door.

"Why are you putting up such a fight if you have nothing to hide, Cask?" demanded Sergeant Byron.

"Being innocent hasn't been reason enough for you not to clap others in irons[93]," my father bellowed, keeping up the struggle.

My Uncle Jonah once told me that you should judge a man not by how he fights when he's winning but when he knows he's going to lose. And father showed no sign of giving up

---

93   Put them in chains/lock them up.

the struggle.

The sergeant strode forward and pulled up my father's shirt, revealing the dressed bayonet-wound. With triumph in his eyes, he looked at my father. "We meet at last, *Captain*," he said, almost spitting out the name my father uses by night.

"Captain?" said my father, still struggling. "I don't know what you mean by that, sergeant, but if a captain I be, I outrank you!" With that, he aimed a swift kick at Byron, the tip of his boot missing the sergeant's shin by a fraction.

Byron stepped back. "You'll be put before the magistrate and a jury of your peers and all will be fair and above board, Cask!" Sergeant Byron insisted. "Justice will be seen to be done! But, with all that contraband stored in the cave at Hangman's Cove, we'll have enough evidence against you to see you hang."

"Justice?" cried Eliza from the open front doorway. "What do you know about Justice? The King's Men, indeed. You're a disgrace to the uniform, the lot of you! I've heard tell of your wild nights of drinking in Fowle and of your –"

"Enough, Eliza," said my father, looking her in the eye. The soldier had managed to get my father's hands behind his back and was forcing him to bend forwards.

But Eliza was not done. She went up to the redcoat grasping my father's wrist and began

hitting him on the back, again and again. Hard. "Don't you try to be avoiding my gaze, Tobias Smart, you Jack of Legs⁹⁴!" she said. "I knew you when you didn't have so much as a sleeve to wipe your snot-nose on, and no fancy uniform is going to change that. I reckon you

---

94   Very tall person.

only took the shilling[95] to be sure to get some clothes to fit! How does your ma feel about you raising your hand against good, honest seafaring folk, what with your own father – God rest his soul – having died a fisherman at sea?"

"Enough, you old bagpipe[96]," said Byron, and went to hit her with the butt of the rifle slung about his neck[97].

---

95 Taking the King's Shilling meant signing up to join the armed forces. If you could be tricked into taking the King's shilling, you could end up being forced into the army or navy. Being forced into the navy was called being pressganged.
96 A long-winded talker.
97 Rifles at this time were loaded through the barrel: gunpowder (to propel the shot), and little metal balls –combining to create the shot – the actual ammunition.

No sooner was the rifle raised than both myself and Sovereign launched ourselves to dear Eliza's defence: me from the stairs and Sovereign from the hearth. Both of us snarled: he in Cornish-Dog and me in English. Father can look after himself, but my dear Eliza?

NO!

The rifle butt intended for Eliza now came into contact with Sovereign's jaw.

I went wild and off the hooks.[98]

Which is how I became the one other arrested with my father and carted off to Fowle.

I'll bet news has spread quicker than the pox[99] and that no-one in Minnock is talking of anything else.

---

98   Crazy.
99   A highly infectious disease.

God knows how many days we've been in this stinking jail cell and He's not telling. James Treppen has been to visit and says that Sovereign is fine. The Reverend Glass is on speaking terms with the witch who lives all on her ownsome between Minnock and Cartsbay. She is an animal healer and has, so Master James tells it, made a poultice from herbs and a special concoction to mend poor Sovereign's jaw.

"She says it'd heal quicker if it were summer and she could use fresh herbs," James Treppen explained, "but that dried herbs will do just as well over time." He then added, as an afterthought, that she's also been looking after Tom Tregowan's leg and some other fellow who'd hurt his head.

"Please thank the Reverend and the witch," I said.

We were calling to each other through a smaller barred window near the top of the door, but neither of us was tall enough to look through it and see the other.

"Reverend Glass says she's not a witch but a healer," said James. "That she could probably be a doctor if women were allowed to be doctors."[100]

I gave a mirthless laugh, not at the thought of a woman having the skills to be a doctor but the likelihood of men ever letting a woman be one. James hadn't only brought news of Sovereign's treatment, but also food, for which we were most grateful. I say 'we' for I am sharing this cell with my father.

---

100   Before being a doctor was seen as a 'proper profession', healing was often carried out by women but, as science progressed and it gained status, women were side-lined and men became 'proper' doctors.

I could not have survived without him. Though to many in Fowle he is just another fisherman from the nearby village of Minnock, here in the jailhouse, he is not without friends. They have brought us blankets – for it's very cold at night in here without a fire – and even a full bottle of rum found its way to my father's lips. But the food is bread, bread and yet more bread, each piece more stale than the last.

James brought us rough-cut slices of cooked meats, which he reached up and stuck through the bars. Just the smell on my fingers from touching it was delicious, so I licked them before tearing off pieces of meat and putting them in my mouth, savouring each mouthful. He also brought paper, ink and quill to write with – they are what I'm using now – and a message for my father from Uncle Jonah.

It was not writ on paper but passed from Uncle Jonah's lips to James Treppen's lips to my father's ear. It was a single word: *Palores*.

Day 44

Today, we were visited by a man dressed all in black, a red skull cap on his head. He wore the biggest gold cross – not crucifix[101] – I have ever seen on a chain around anyone's neck. He had a look of absolute peace upon his face but, when he tilted forward, it was obscured by great locks of hair as white as Cotswold lions.[102] With him was a fellow clergyman, who could not have been less like him if he'd tried. Whereas the first man was all straight lines, flowing robes and neatness, the second was all sharp angles: jutting elbows and knees, with hair like an abandoned bird's nest, left to the elements. Most unusual for a parson, he also had a beard in as much disarray as an untamed hedgerow in summer. This smaller, messy, man was clutching a battered black leather-bound Bible.

---

101   A crucifix includes Christ on the cross.
102   Slang for sheep.

When the jailer let them into our cell, he
raised an eyebrow to my father. "Never had
you down as a religious man, Jon Cask," he

said, "but the fear of the drop[103] is enough to turn any man to God, I suppose."

"I'm as God-fearing as any man, Rod Tundy," my father replied, "and I have every faith that I shall not hang."

"Then you're more of an ass than the law itself![104]" said the jailer with a chuckle. He stepped out of the cell, slamming the thick wooden door behind him, and there was a jangle of keys as he locked us all in. "Call me when you're ready, Father."

No sooner had Rod Tundy's footsteps faded down the flag-stoned corridor, than my father threw his arms around the black-robed Reverend, who hugged him back. It was then I noticed the tip of an anchor tattoo upon his wrist, sticking out beneath his cuff.

I knew then all was not what it seemed, for I've never seen black-cattle[105] with a tattoo!

---

103   Being hanged.
104   The phrase "the law is an ass" wasn't used by Charles Dickens until the nineteenth century, but "the law is such an ass" appeared in the seventeenth century, and the jailer is expressing similar sentiments between the two, in the eighteenth!
105   Clergymen/parsons.

A moment later, off came the golden cross and chain, the hat and the wig and, there before me, stood a redcoat… at least, the man was dressed in the King's men uniform.

I was aghast. What did all this mean?

Before I had time to think more of it, my father said, "Get dressed, Kitty," and I saw the second man – a lad – had also slipped from his disguise. He was dressed like one of the boys who ran messages for the soldiers for the odd farthing.[106]

"Good to see you, Silas," said my father to the 'redcoat'.

"This is my boy, Christopher," said the man.

My father smiled and nodded in his direction. "And may St Christopher protect us on our journey out of here, for, though few in steps, it's as fraught in as many dangers as the roughest sea."[107]

The black robe, wig and red-cap fitted Father perfectly, and the smaller so-called parson's clothes were an excellent fit for me. My father tilted his head forward and the wig obscured his features and, anyway, all eyes would be on that enormous golden cross.

---

106   A farthing was the coin of least value: Two farthings made a ha'penny; two ha'pennies made a penny; twelve pennies made a shilling; two-and-a-half shillings made half-a-crown, two half-crowns made a crown; two crowns made ten shillings; two ten shillings made a pound; one pound and one shilling made a guinea. (So 12 pennies = 1 shilling; 20 shillings = 1 pound.)

107   A Christian legend has it that a giant of a man was carrying people across a swollen river but, when it came to carrying a tiny child to safety, he found it hard because the child weighed so much. When he successfully reached the far bank, he discovered that the child was Jesus Christ and he'd weighed so much because he was carrying the weight of the world on his shoulders. The man was Christopher. He became, for a time, Saint Christopher, Patron Saint of Travelling.

"Practise the walk, all elbows and knees," my father instructed, which I did across the cell floor with such success that he grinned with glee. "First time, my splendid Kitty!" he said.

With my bird's-nest 'hair' and 'beard', clutching the leather-bound Bible and walking the angular walk, I couldn't have looked less like Kitty Cask if I tried.

"What now?" I whispered.

"We bid farewell to this Godforsaken place!"

With that, Silas, the so-called priest now dressed as a so-called soldier, called out to Rod Tundy in his most priestly tone, "Guard? Guard?"

We heard a grunt and shuffle and a jangling of keys getting nearer and nearer as the jailer padded down the corridor. "Coming, Reverend!" he called. I then heard him distinctly mutter. "Guard? Guard? I ain't no guard me, I'm chief jailer…"

He peered through the small barred window in the cell door and saw me and father in our religious disguises. Silas and his boy Christopher were flat against the wall that shared the doorway, keeping out of sight. There was the sound of the key in the lock, more jangling of keys, and the cell door opened. He stepped inside then stepped aside to less us pass, which is when Silas knocked him unconscious from behind. As quick as a flash, he and Christopher dragged the sleeping jailer to a corner. The lad took some sturdy string from his pocket and, before he could

say, "Help me!" they had him trussed up like a
Christmas goose.[108]

"Ready?" asked Father, looking every bit the
clergyman.

"One moment," said Silas, reaching up into
the back of his jacket. He pulled out a redcoat's
hat and placed it on his head. "Ready," he said.

---

108   'Trussed up' means tied up and, as for goose, this was a far more
      popular bird at Christmas than turkey in eighteenth century Britain.

And so it was that a priest – with an eye-catching cross that kept all eyes off his face – accompanied by a parson – with a strange enough walk to make any prison guard try not to grin – left Fowle Jail in the company of a redcoat and his messenger boy. An unusual and interesting sight, but not enough to raise the slightest suspicion!

Had anyone troubled to follow us out through the main gate, across the square and down the alleyway, they might have been surprised, however, to see us all step into the back of a carriage together, to be driven off in the direction of Minnock at high speed.

"You knew they were coming?" I asked my father as we rattled along.

"I knew Jonah had arranged some form of escape, yes."

"But not what it was?"

"No, though he did give me a clue as to what to look out for."

"Palores?" I asked.

"Palores," he nodded.

That had been the one-word message from my uncle to my father: *Palores*. It's the Cornish word for the chough[109], a bird, and means 'digger' because that's what choughs do...

109 Pronounced 'chuff', these birds had all but disappeared from Cornwall by the early 1950s but are now making a comeback.

But why, then, didn't it mean that we were to dig a tunnel out of jail, or that they were digging in to free us?

I thought some more.

The chough even appears on the Cornish coat of arms[110], atop a crown. It is like a mighty crow – a black bird – with red beak and… Aha! Silas had dressed as a priest in *black* robe and *red* cap, like a chough!

And then I remembered the old legend of the Cornish chough. "The story goes that when King Arthur died he turned into a bird, with red beak and legs to represent his bloody end, and took flight!" I said.

"Clever girl!" said Father with a proud grin.

"So, when you saw the priest in the black robe and red cap you knew that you – the king, the captain – would turn into him and take flight from the jail!"

Father nodded. "Your Uncle Jonah loves a

---

110 Today's coat-of-arms shows a sailor supporting one side of the shield and a miner supporting the other but still includes a chough. This wasn't the official coat of arms for Cornwall in Kitty's day, where the chough featured even more prominently.

puzzle and has a way with words," he said, "but I don't know if he knows a priest in red cap is a cardinal, one of the Pope's right-hand men." He laughed. "I rather doubt a cardinal would come to see us, especially when we're not even papists![111]"

"If only we could now work out who betrayed us," said Silas, and we all-four fell silent once more.

With thanks and promises exchanged, Father had us put down at the crossroads by Monkswood, and the carriage continued its journey without us. With our disguises discarded, we were fisherman and daughter once more: wanted by the law, no doubt, but less conspicuous across country than a couple of clergy!

---

111   Another word for Roman Catholics.

"What now?" I asked.

"Now, Kitty? You have a chance to put your skills to the test. I have a task for you I can entrust to no one else."

"Not even Jago?"

"Jago is the wrong – er – build for such an important task. And now is the time for you to put all that creeping about in the dark to good use."

"Anything, Father." I would always have followed my father to the ends of the Earth but, having been responsible for his injury, I now feel even more indebted to him.

"The evidence against us is the huge store of

smuggled goods within that cave," he said.

Silas had told us in our hurried coach-ride that the redcoats had also stored all the goods they had salvaged after the fight in the cave which they now guarded, along with all the goods father already had stored there.

"But what can I do?" I asked. "It'll be riddled with redcoats!"

"Which is why it is the last place in Cornwall they'd expect either of us to turn up!" said Father, that old twinkle returning to his eye.

"But how –?" How did he expect to remove fifty or sixty barrels or crates from underneath their noses?

"The redcoats came from the cave when they attacked us, which means that they came down the secret passage into the cave after we'd done the same and were on the beach," he said. "So, if they're guarding the cave, they'll have posted men at the cave mouth in case anyone comes in by sea, and at the entrance to the passage. But I'll wager that they know nothing of the blowhole!"

"Blowhole?" I asked.

Father took a stick and drew a diagram of the cave in the mud. It looked not dissimilar to this:

"The cave was made by the sea," my father explained. "Given enough time, water can wear away the weaknesses in rock. At high tide the water would have come crashing in, building up pressure, making a hole in the top like a whale's blowhole, water spraying skywards!"

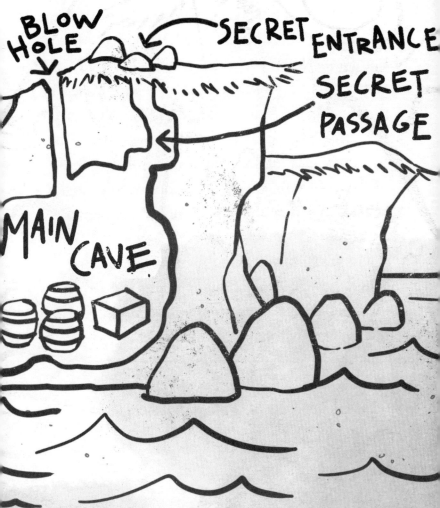

BLOW HOLE

SECRET ENTRANCE

SECRET PASSAGE

MAIN CAVE

My father's Uncle Edward – my great uncle – had left Cornwall for the Americas and sailed on whaling vessels from New Bedford in New England, near the famous whaling town of Nantucket. When he retired and paid a visit home, a much changed and bragging man, he told many tales of these leviathans[112] of the sea. About how the whales were harpooned – like a giant spear on a rope and chain – dragged back to port, its fatty blubber cut off[113] and boiled in giant caldrons[114], to separate the oil to be used for lamps and greasing machinery. He said that the smell was terrible, but I was thinking more of the poor whale, with its bones used to make everything from the ribs of ladies' corsets to fishing rods.

My great uncle had told stories of chasing down the whales and seeing water spew from their blowholes when they surfaced in the sea, giving their whereabouts away.

---

112   Huge sea creatures referred to in the Bible.
113   The process is called flensing.
114   Called trypots.

"But why doesn't the sea still fill the cave and spew through the hole?" I asked.

"I reckon it's because, over time, it's washed more and more sand and shingle and rocks onto the beach making it higher and higher so the water can no longer reach so far. I've seen whole coves change their appearance after one mighty storm. Who knows? One day the cave may flood again.[115] But, in the meantime, I need you to climb down that blowhole into the

---

115   Sometimes the silting up of estuaries or changing of coastlines was blamed on other forces, such as angered merpeople (mermaids AND mermen).

cave, set the gunpowder, light the fuse and get back out of there."

My heart beat faster at the word *gunpowder*; at the thought of the explosion; at the very *danger* of it all; and with pride, that Father should intrust such an important task to

ME.

"I come back up through the blowhole?"

He nodded. "Back up through the blowhole. And blow up all the contraband which is the only real evidence they have against us."

"But why me?"

"You are my daughter, Kitty," said my father. "There is no one I trust more than you to carry out this vital task. I would do it myself if it weren't for my injury."

We sat in a hollow surrounded by gorse bushes, protecting us from prying eyes, going over the plan time and time again. When it was dark, we made our way to the point where we would have to part company and meet again if all went well.

"If they catch you, don't resist," he said. "I mean it. Simply give yourself up to them. They won't harm a hair on your head. You need to be much more wary of the gunpowder than of the redcoats. You will be a valuable asset to them because they know that I'll give myself up in exchange for your freedom. And if that does happen –" he paused and grinned "– I'll simply find another way to get free!"

"I shall go as quietly as a lamb," I assured him, imagining a snarling, biting, kicking lamb that would be no one's prisoner.

He had told me specific markers to look out for in the dark that would lead me to the blow hole – a pile of stones here; a dead hawthorn tree there; the gorse bushes growing close like a hedge. I turned left and right, along and up and down, crouching low to limit my chances of being spotted by any redcoats guarding the clifftop entrance to the secret passage in the cave.

Finally, I came to a large flat rock, almost surrounded by gorse. Gorse is prickly. I've always known that but now I *know* it. Squeezing between those thorns was painful, but it was my father's neck at stake here. The rock – like a large stone slab – was heavy but I managed to push it to one side. The hole it revealed looked down into utter blackness. The one good thing about this was that it meant that there were no guards below, sitting inside the cave with lanterns. I felt around for the knotted rope that my father had assured me was attached to an iron ring fitted securely to the roof of the cave to the side of the hole. I took a hold of it and, saying a quick prayer, lowered myself in.

The thing that frightened me most as I made my way down was not the fear of being caught. It was not the dangers of using the gunpowder and timing it just right to get out again. It was the fear of not knowing where the rope would end. Would it be below the next knot or the next, or would I be lowering myself and lowering myself…

…And finally I found my feet touching the sandy floor. I was flooded with relief.

I crouched a while, staring in the direction of where I took the mouth of the cave to be, allowing my eyes to adjust to what little light there was.

Now, I had to follow my father's instructions to the letter. I found my way to the back wall and felt my way along at shoulder height for an alcove in the rocks where, he had told me, I would find a lantern and a tinderbox. The lantern was shielded on all but one side, he said, so, hold it correctly and it wouldn't shine in the direction of the front of the cave where the redcoats were probably stationed. It took me a few turns of walking beside the wall, feeling along the rock, but eventually I found the alcove. I had no difficulty creating a spark and lighting the tinder and then the lantern. At last, I could see the stretch of sandy floor before me. I studied what I saw with interest, and not just where it led.

Father had told me to find a small cask of gunpowder, about the size of the one Betty Polegate had hidden beneath her skirt at The Black Eye. It was marked with a red 'X' and had a bung in the side, and would be on top of one of the much larger barrels, also marked 'X'.

I carefully placed the lantern at a safe distance, on a crate marked FINEST SILKS, removed the bung from the cask, and walked around the cluster of bigger barrels, pouring gunpowder from the hole, creating a circle of black powder around them. I then walked backwards, turning the 'O' of powder into a 'Q' with a very long tale indeed.

What I needed to make sure was that the trail was long enough to give me time to get up the rope and out of there. I was beginning to realise that this could well be a problem. Of course, I could lead the trail of powder to the bottom of the rope, climb half way up it, then throw the lantern down to light it, but I quickly saw three problems:

1. I'd have to climb much of the rope whilst

clutching the lantern, which was nigh on impossible.

2. The lantern may go out when it hit the ground, rather than igniting the gunpowder trail.

3. The crash of the lantern hitting the ground might attract redcoats who'd have time to stop the flame reaching the bigger barrel of gunpowder.

I muttered a few mild curses under my breath. What then? What had my father been thinking? Maybe because he knew the cave so much better than I did, he assumed I'd find my way around to leave a lot longer trail of powder: the tail to the 'Q'?

Then I had an idea. I took off my shirt and tore it into strips, tucking the ends into the top of my trousers. It was time to get out of here.

As ready as I'd ever be, with the gunpowder trail ending in another circle, filled in with the black powder this time, based at the foot of the rope, I grasped the rope and began my climb. Fortunately, I'd counted the number of knots in the rope on the way *down*, so I'd have an idea of how near the top I was on the way up. When I was three-quarters of the way up, I wrapped myself around the rope as best I could and took out the tinderbox. I fumbled it between my fingers and almost dropped it, my heart in my mouth, but managed to hold it tight. Then I created a spark and a flame. I set fire to each strip of my torn shirt in quick succession, let the flame take hold and dropped it.

I needed just one to remain alight by the time it had reached the bottom and for it to ignite the gunpowder trail... And it worked.

I could hear the sizzling of the powder down below as I pulled myself from the blowhole and, crouching low, ran for my dear life.

Far greater than even my father had expected. Lucky that I ran and ran and ran because it not only destroyed all evidence of contraband but it also brought the cave down. I watched as a huge plume of fire burst though the blowhole, then rock flew everywhere, and the ground gave way and the cave caved in. The noise was deafening and the silence after it was like no silence I have ever known. Then I heard shouts. Not cries of pain, but shouts of surprise and panic and orders amongst the redcoats on the beach below. I stayed low, fearful that the ground may give away beneath me, though I was on solid ground.

I felt triumphant and dazed and hoping that no redcoat – however much I hate them – had been caught in the blast.

I felt a hand upon my shoulder and turned. I could make out the form of my father.

"I think we can call that a success," he said. And laughed.

Day 41

I did not think my father could have been prouder than he was when the cave and its contents were destroyed and I emerged unharmed. But then, later last night, I told him what I had seen in the sandy floor, when I first lit the lantern.

"I thought at first that it was the mark of a walking stick or cane, and gave it little thought," I told him,

"then I realised that it was the dots of the go-dot-and-carry… the little round circles left in the sand by the end of a wooden leg."

"But –" began my father.

"But," I interrupted, "I remember you telling me that Jack Treviss has never *been* in the cave. You've always used him as a lookout because he could slow the human chain passing cargo from ship to shore to cave."

"And no honest smuggler would disobey me for fear of being followed and giving away our hideaway!" said my father with a nod.

"So do you think –?"

"Yes. Kitty, I do think," said my father, Jon Cask, the Captain. "I think you have just uncovered our traitor. The spy… who you've been calling the viper in the nest."

"WE'VE GOT HIM!"

I said, my eyes shining in triumph. Then my face fell. "But maybe too late."

My father held me close. "No," he said. "Not too late. Not too late at all. I have a plan."

He gave me a squeeze in his great big arms. "Kitty Cask," he said. "Your mother would be so proud of you. As, of course, am I."

No other words could have made me happier than these.

Day 44

I have learned much these last few days. Not least that the tale of our daring escape is the talk of Cornwall, though it has become more and more outrageous at each retelling. The latest version, I am told, is that we left the jail with my father dressed as the Bishop of Bath and Wells, accompanied by a whole platoon of soldiers! One thing of which there is no doubt, and is impossible to exaggerate, is Rod Tundy's

RAGE

at having been tricked, knocked unconscious and made prisoner in his own jail!

But all that has paled into insignificance compared to the 'daring raid on the cave at Hangman's Cove'. Apparently, a group of masked men, all dressed in black, had abseiled down the cliff on ropes, taken the redcoats by surprise, and blown-up the cave and all its contents.

Little did they know that it was the work of but one girl!

The next part of the plan surprised me. Father went with me and the Reverend Glass to Fowle to see the magistrate, Sir William Boyle, to give himself up.

YES:
G-I-V-E H-I-M-S-E-L-F U-P.

He took with him a sworn statement, dictated to the parson, from Robert Tregowan, stating that my father, Jon Cask, had received the wound to his side when he, Robert, had stabbed him in a drunken brawl at The Black Eye; an attack witnessed by everyone there that evening, including the landlord and landlady,

the Polegates, and all of whom were prepared to swear it also.

My father freely admitted the offence of escaping jail, but that he had been wrongly imprisoned and concerned for the safety of me, his daughter. But, that aside, he argued, he had done nothing against the law, him being nothing more than a God-fearing Cornishman, and widower, who made his livelihood by fishing! All that had been hurt had been Rod Tundy's pride.

He was accused of being a smuggler, but where was the evidence? He had never been arrested at the scene of any smuggling.

No stolen goods had been found in his house, his fishing boat or any other place with which he was associated; all of which had been thoroughly searched. So, on what basis was Mr Duggan and Sergeant Byron making all these claims?

"I am, of course, more than happy to face a jury of my peers," he said, "but there is no case to answer, Sir William, and it would be wasting yours and the court's time."

News must have reached Mr Duggan's office at the harbour that my father was with Sir William and, with a knock, he entered the magistrate's office. He nodded at the Reverend Glass but chose to ignore me and my father.

"Sir William –" he began.

Seated at his desk, the signed statement from Robert Tregowan before him, the magistrate gave the exciseman a long, hard stare, and explained what my father had told him. "And what," he said at last, "is your response to that, Mr Duggan?"

"We have no contraband as evidence because Cask destroyed it all, sir," he protested, "and –"

"You have evidence that this explosion was by the hand of this man?" asked the magistrate, pointing to my father.

"Well, no, sir, but it was obviously carried out on his instruction."

"And why should anyone carry out his instructions?" demanded Sir William.

"Because… Because he is the notorious Captain, responsible for all the smuggling in Minnock, sir," said Mr Duggan, his face reddening.

"I look forward to the proof, Duggan," said the magistrate. "And I mean now. Not at trial. Well, where is it, man?"

"The proof is the word of Mr Jack Treviss," said Mr Duggan, finding it impossible to keep the triumph from his voice. "I have asked that Sergeant Byron bring him here this instant to give testimony."

"And why should we take the word of Jack Treviss over that of Mr Cask?" asked the Reverend Glass. "I wish to speak ill of no man, but old Jack is a retired one-legged sailor whose love of tall tales[116] is only surpassed by his love of ale."

"A one-legged man, yes," said Duggan, "but no drunkard. He is in my employ and his so-called love of drink is nothing more than an act; a pretence. He is in the official employ of –"

---

116   Made-up or exaggerated stories.

At that moment, the door swung open and the go-dot-and-carry – that treacherous wooden-legged traitor – came lurching into the room, closely followed by a very flustered-looking Sergeant Byron. The smell of brandy reached us before they did.

"Sir William," began the redcoat. "I really must apologise, but –"

"Hello, whisker-face!" said Jack Treviss, slapping his hands on the table in front of the magistrate then tugging his whiskers. "Who's a handsome fellow? You are.

YES YOOOOOOOU!"

He gave a terrible belch of such force that he seemed to lose his balance and, spinning for a moment on his wooden leg, landed flat on his back. He pointed skyward. "Nice ceiling, your whiskership!" he yelled.

"Enough!" said Sir William, getting to his feet. "I have had quite enough of this, Duggan. This is your spy, is it? This is the professional in your employ who only pretends to be drunk and is the only thing between Jon Cask and the gallows, is it? Well. I've had enough, I say. You *and* you, Sergeant Byron, are to leave Mr Cask, his daughter… his entire *family* alone, and let him go about his lawful business without so much as 'good morning'. If I hear that either of you has so much as raised a hat in greeting to him or let his name pass your lips I'll have YOU in court."

The magistrate's face was beginning to glow dangerously red. "As for Mr Jack Whatever-His-Name-May-Be here," he pointed at the drunk sailor on his floor. "No honest man can afford to drink that much brandy with all the taxes we pay on top, so I suggest you search HIS lodgings for any contraband, taking my constable with you, and report straight back to me."

And that was that.

No charges brought against my father.

His name cleared.

The authorities warned off.

I don't know whether to laugh or to burst into song!

We are now all free, and with no small thanks to me, for it was me who blew up the cave and it was me who exposed one-legged Jack Treviss as the spy, though I can't take credit for making him drink all that drink or for hiding all those boxes of tea – taken from the secret cellar – in his rooms, for the constable to find, of course.

I no longer think of myself as Kitty Cask, Smuggler's Daughter, though, for we – Father, Jago, Esme and old Eliza, who claims that my sister "will need her" – have decided to start a new life, free of smuggling and trying to outwit the law, in the Americas, and our boat leaves in three weeks time.

And, of course, Sovereign will be coming also. Fully recovered, he too played his part against those dastardly redcoats and is much a member of the family as I!

Who knows – perhaps I will start a new diary about life not in the West Country, but in the wild Wild West! But, wherever I might end up, I will always be a Cornishwoman, through and through. It is in my bones and blood.

AND
NEXT...?

There is little doubt that the Reverend Glass was somehow involved in Jon Cask's smuggling ring but, because Kitty did not know or, at least, didn't record it in her diary, we have no way of knowing. We do know that smuggling continued in Minnock, long after the Casks left for America, with a new landing spot a little further down the coast and that, when the Reverend Glass retired, he was far richer than one might expect a clergyman to be. He was much loved by the people of Minnock, though, because, even in old age – when James Treppen was squire after his father was killed in a riding accident – he gave much to help the poor and needy of the parish. Mr Duggan remained an exciseman, feared throughout Cornwall, and was very successful at catching freetraders everywhere but Minnock. He stayed well away from there and the memories of those who'd out-witted him. Kitty's Uncle Jonah remained in the village, living to the extraordinary age of 102, where he regaled with tales about the antics of his infamous family, always giving Kitty credit

where credit was due. And as for the Casks?
In America, the Land of Opportunity, they
became fine, upstanding citizens. Apparently.

SMUGGLING IN THE WEST COUNTRY IN THE EIGHTEENTH CENTURY

We do know that a number of eighteenth century West Country clergymen were involved in smuggling: sometimes actively, sometimes helping to hide the contraband on Church property, or sometimes simply agreeing to turn a blind eye in return for a few goods. In some instances, whole villages seem to be involved in smuggling. Poverty in the West Country was very serious and the taxes on goods were very unpopular, so smuggling was a way of earning money to put food on the table and a roof over your head, and enjoying a better quality of life. Not that it was limited to the poor. Squires, doctors, and magistrates in many towns and villages were all involved in smuggling, or knew full well who was responsible and benefitted from cheaper goods. Some towns and villages ran small-time operations, others ran it like big business, moving thousands of pounds worth of goods a year, playing cat-and-mouse with the authorities and the redcoats.

A NOTE FROM THE AUTHOR

ONLY
THE
FACTS
ARE TRUE

Although none of the characters in this book are real and there is no Hangman's Cove, Cannon's Point, village of Minnock or town of Fowle, smuggling really was a way of life for many in the eighteenth century in the West Country of England, as the story shows.

Another great way to bring smuggling history to life is, of course, to visit a National Trust coastline, explore the coves and caves and winding lanes, and to look out to sea and imagine…

Philip Ardagh